THE SIXTH
(OR SEVENTH)
MAN

By

Alexander McCall Smith

Illustrations by Iain McIntosh

MACLEAN DUBOIS

Published in Edinburgh, 2012, in an edition limited to 1000 copies.

MACLEAN DUBOIS, Hillend House, Hillend, Edinburgh

Printed by THE UNIVERSITY OF EDINBURGH PRINTING SERVICES

This is for Joseph Kanon

1. There has been a great deal of discussion about the order of these men. One way of approaching the issue is to name them in the order of their unmasking, which gives Burgess and Maclean the first two positions, while Philby, the more elusive and consummate spy, occupies the third. Blunt, who might claim a higher position chronologically, in this scheme becomes the Fourth Man, and Cairncross, who evaded publicity in sybaritic retirement in France, is relegated to the obscurity of the fifth position. But who was the sixth? The Sixth Man is mentioned in no spy-catcher memoirs nor is he so much as a footnote in those bulky histories of espionage that fall from the presses every year. His name was Fergus Andrew Mactavish and he was a farmer on the Ardnamurchan peninsula of Argyll. He went to his grave, unexposed, in 2003. At that simple ceremony of farewell, conducted under a West Highland sky filled with sharp, April light, only two of those present were aware of any claim that Fergus might have to be listed in the company of those infamous spies. And those two would never speak about it. Never.

2. Mactavish – as he was generally known – had a farm not far from Ardgour, a village on the shores of Loch Linnhe, a long sea loch that led up to Fort William and the Great Glen beyond.

Ardgour did not consist of very much – a hotel, well-placed at the top of the ferry slipway, a general shop, and a post office. But that was all that most people needed. For any other purpose there was Fort William a brief ferry ride and drive away, or Oban about an hour or so further south. Above the village there were great sweeps of mountainside down which, after heavy rain, thin waterfalls fell like white threads. It was dramatic scenery by any standards, but taken for granted, as such things always are, by those who lived there. The mountains, though beautiful, supported very few sheep; the waterfalls and lochs were all very well but they led to the general damp that brought the midges in their summer swarms; and the sea loch cut one off from places that would otherwise have been more easily reached. Yet it was clearly was far better than Glasgow, where people went off in search of work, only to find that they yearned for everything they had left behind, and from which they often returned, determined not to leave again.

3. Mactavish's farm was barely two hundred acres, but was large enough to support a small herd of beef cattle and a flock of Scotch Blackface sheep. He was a good farmer, and made the most of things, as had his wife, who had died when their daughter, Kirsty, was seventeen. Kirsty remained at home, not entirely out of a sense of duty, but because she saw no reason to go anywhere else. This suited Mactavish, as she was a good housekeeper, but he occasionally wondered what would happen if she were to marry. He hoped that she would do so, of course, as he wanted her to be happy, and he belonged to a generation where to be single was seen as a failure significantly reducing one's chances of happiness.

But she showed no signs of looking for a husband, smiling enigmatically whenever he tactfully mentioned the possibility. "You never know," she said. "Maybe I will, maybe I won't. And there aren't all that many decent men around here, if you ask me. So maybe I won't."

4. In 1980, when Mactavish was fifty-four and Kirsty was twenty-seven, there was a major crisis in their household. This concerned land and came about when the local council declared its intention of slicing off a portion of Mactavish's best field in order to build a new road.

"Nobody needs a new road," Mactavish pointed out in a long and outraged letter to his councillor.

"Probably not," replied the councillor. "I certainly voted against it, but it's the committee, you see. They're the ones who look after roads and things like that. They said we do need a road, and that's that. You'll get your compensation, remember."

That, thought Mactavish, was not the point. He wanted land, not money, and he vigorously protested his case to this effect, even engaging a solicitor in Inverness to write on his behalf to the council. His efforts were to no avail, though, and he concluded that that the British state, as represented by its road-making authorities in the Western Highlands, was rotten to the core.

Tossing and turning in his bed one night, filled with resentment at the imminent arrival of the council's bulldozers, it occurred to him that if the authorities could treat a law-abiding farmer in such a way then they had sacrificed any claim they might have to his loyalty. And it was at that point, just as he was about to get up to attend to the livestock, that he decided he would work for the Soviet Union. That would teach them, he thought. That would teach them up in Inverness. That would teach them in Edinburgh and London. They would have only themselves to blame.

5. The *Oban Times* had reported in considerable detail the exposure of Anthony Blunt, and Mactavish was amongst those readers who had followed the case with some interest. He had read about controllers and meetings in London parks. He had read about the Soviet Union's seemingly insatiable appetite for information about military arrangements; well, he thought, Loch Linnhe was a waterway of some importance: you could take a submarine up as far as Fort William if you really wanted to, and that, in fact, might be just the sort of thing that the Soviet Union might wish to do. The *Oban Times* had once reported Russian submarines being sighted off Skye, and that was not all that far away. If you were prowling around Skye in a submarine then it might be quite convenient to be able to slip into Loch Linnhe for a day or two and rest while British submarines looked for you in the Sound of Mull. You would have to be careful, though, that you didn't try to cross the route taken by the Corran Ferry, because the loch was not all that deep at that point and the last thing you'd want would be for your conning tower to be clipped by the ferry's propeller.

Mactavish thought about all this, and then, in a sudden moment of decision, he obtained a copy of the Corran Ferry timetable. This he placed in an envelope with a covering note, and, having obtained the address of the Soviet Embassy in London from a telephone directory in the Fort William Public Library, posted it.

The covering note said: *I am prepared to work for you. This information could be helpful for submarine activity. Please contact me for further assistance. Yours truly, F.A. Mactavish.*

6. Kirsty noticed that her father seemed somewhat jumpy over the days that followed. He had not mentioned his act of treason to her, of course, and she had no idea why he showed such interest in the arrival of the postmistress in her van.

"Are you expecting something?" she said. "A cheque maybe?"

Mactavish shook his head. "No," he said. "Nothing." Even as he spoke, the thought crossed his mind: *How very easy it is to lie. That's what those people did. Philby and the others. They were very good liars.*

After a week of waiting, he began to feel anxious. What if the letter had been intercepted by the authorities? What if the intelligence people in London had steamed it open and found the Corran Ferry timetable and his offer to work for the Soviets? He had put his address at the top of his letter and so they would have no difficulty tracing him. Perhaps that was a mistake. Perhaps he should have arranged a meeting at what the *Oban Times* had described as a "drop-off point". He swallowed hard. *I'm an amateur,* he thought. *I've made the most fundamental of mistakes.*

The sense of excitement and anticipation that he had felt was now replaced by a gnawing sense of dread. This was compounded by guilt. He had betrayed his country in a fit of anger and now, on more mature reflection, he realised what a terrible thing he had done. His father had served in the Argyll and Sutherland Highlanders, just as his grandfather had done. An uncle had been in the Black Watch and had been commended for his bravery. And here he was, Fergus Mactavish, offering his services to the Soviet Union, about which he knew nothing and which had no claim at all on his loyalty.

He went to see the local Church of Scotland minister. Sitting awkwardly in the minister's study, a cup of tea cooling at his elbow, he confessed what he had done. The minister allowed him to tell the whole story before he said anything.

"You should drink your tea, Mactavish," he said at last. "I can't take cold tea myself – never could."

There was a brief silence. Then the minister continued, "You sent them the ferry timetable, you say?"

Mactavish nodded miserably.

The minister smiled. "I wouldn't worry too much about that, you know. You can get the ferry timetable in the shop."

"But I offered to do more."

The minister raised an eyebrow. "What else could you do? I'm not being rude, but what on earth could you do for the Soviet Union?"

Mactavish stared at the floor. "You don't think it's too bad?"

The minister shook his head. "Come on, man, be sensible! Anybody who heard about this would burst out laughing. Anybody would think it's a great joke. Nobody would take it seriously."

Mactavish left the minister's house feeling as if a great weight had been taken off his shoulders. He returned to the house, where he made a full confession to his daughter.

"I knew there was something biting you," she said. "But I had no idea it would be so ridiculous."

Mactavish said nothing. He wanted now to forget all about it. It was coming up to the lambing season and he would have his hands more than full with his ewes.

7. A month later, a letter arrived from the Soviet Embassy. When Mactavish opened it and saw the headed paper, he gave an involuntary gasp. His daughter, who had just come into the room, looked at him with concern.

"Is that about the road?" she asked.

He handed the letter to her. "It's from the Russians," he said. "They're coming to see me."

She frowned as she read it. "So this Mr Yuri Olevsky is coming next week," she said. "Well, you just go to the police. Speak to Sergeant Cameron."

"I can't do that," Mactavish exclaimed. "I can't go and tell the police that I offered to work for the Soviet Union. Willie Cameron would have to arrest me. I'd be taken off to Inverness Prison before I knew what was happening."

Kirsty thought for a moment. "But they might *turn* you. MI5 or whoever they are might use you as a double agent."

Mactavish dismissed this suggestion. "This is what happens when you do what I did," he said, his voice full of misery. "It's the same as with that fellow, Blunt. You get in too deep and then you can't get out again."

She took her father's hand and held it. He looked at her, lovingly, in gratitude. Family would always forgive; they would forgive wrongs both small and large; meanness, venality, even treason.

"When Mr Olevsky comes," she said quietly, "we'll give him a cup of tea but we must be firm. We shall tell him that you are no longer prepared to serve the Soviet Union."

"I didn't think I ever really began to do that," said Mactavish. "That's what the minister said."

"Well, there you are," said Kirsty. "You can tell him that you're not going to start."

She looked out of the window. A squall had blown in from the south west – a veil of gentle rain, like white mist, moving across the surface of the distant loch. The light behind it had the quality of silver.

8. Yuri Olevsky was in his early thirties – rather younger than they had imagined. He had dark, slicked down hair, which lent him the appearance of a nineteen-thirties dance instructor. He had very white teeth, and regular features. He was very handsome.

They drank tea together. He seemed nervous, and after a few minutes of pleasantries, Mactavish thought that he should not delay in revealing his change of heart.

"With all due respect to the Soviet Union," he said, "I have decided that I do not wish to get involved."

Olevsky looked at him. "This place you have here is very beautiful," he said.

Mactavish inclined his head in recognition of the compliment.

Then Olevsky said, "I am ashamed of my country. I, too, no longer wish to serve it."

Mactavish and his daughter stared at him. Neither knew what to say. Treason, it seemed, unknown in Ardgour since the 1745 Jacobite rebellion – and that wasn't real treason, if you were a

Jacobite – now seemed endemic.

Eventually Mactavish found his voice "Oh," he said. And then he added. "Aye."

"I told my superiors that I was following up a lead in Glasgow," Olevsky continued. "They do not know I am here." He paused. "I should therefore like to apply for political asylum."

Mactavish looked at Kirsty. "What do we do?"

Olevsky intercepted the question. "You fetch the authorities," he said.

Mactavish shrugged his shoulders. "We don't have any authorities up here. There's Willie Cameron, I suppose, but he's not based here. He's at the police office in Strontian."

Now Kirsty acted. "Why don't you just stay with us?" she asked. "You could get work in the hotel – the one down by the ferry. And I know somebody who's looking for somebody to help him on his fishing boat."

Mactavish opened his mouth to protest. She had not asked him how he would feel about having a Russian staying in the house, but then he stopped himself. He looked at his daughter; she was gazing at Olevsky, who was smiling back at her encouragingly.

9. Olevsky proved to be very handy on the fishing boat. He was also a rather good plasterer, and gradually started doing more of that in houses throughout Lochaber. He and Kirsty married eight months later, and began work on a bungalow for themselves a few hundred yards from Mactavish's farmhouse, in exactly the spot where the road was to have been built. That plan had been scrapped as the council had experienced a budgetary deficit and

had other, more pressing needs to attend to. For Macavish, that was a victory that gave him immense satisfaction.

Two grandsons were born over the next four years. Olevsky loved to dress his sons in kilts and shower them with gifts sent over from his aunts in Leningrad. When the Soviet Union fell, these aunts came to Scotland for a holiday and brought even more gifts for the boys. They invited Mactavish to visit them in St Petersburg, which he did with enthusiasm. The aunts told him about the popularity of Robert Burns in Russian translation. "He speaks to the Russian soul," they said. "He really does."

Olevsky framed a copy of the Corran Ferry timetable and hung it on the wall of their kitchen. People commented on this odd choice of decoration, but he said nothing to divulge the reason behind it. Training in the keeping of secrets often survives a change in one's circumstances.

In the summer, on warm days, he and Kirsty, accompanied by their two sons, would follow a path up to a pool at the bottom of one of the waterfalls. They would swim in the bracing clear water and then, while the boys played at the edge of the pool, the parents would lie back in the heather and look up at the sky, on such days cloudless, a pale blue witness to their happiness.